YOURSELF

EVERYTHING FOR LIFE

JAFRENA

<u>**looking forward for the best???**</u>

its YOU

Contents

Stephen Haw

Albert Einstein

Foreword

power

Preface

yourself

"

ONE
A FAIIRYTALE

"BY THE WORD FAIRYTALE, EVERYONE CAN IMAGINE THE beautiful THINGS THAT NOBODY GONNA IMAGINE."

live is totally a fairytale?YES,cause the more you get thoughts the more you gonna acheive.dont just dream about unbelievable things,sure you can try out which gonna work out.you may be sad or happy or depends!!but everything which feels negative life sadness,depression kindof things is not at all permnent.the positive vides are totally permanent.if your religious tust your god if not trust what you wanna do.but the thinhg is TRUST and HOPE are common for eveyone.

not everyone in this world getting whaterver they want.if you want something work yourself work. no billinores came out sleeping or lazy.the work you do on yourself is the result you are going to get.

eveything comes into our life is lessons like stories and chapters.either the chapter will have good end or it might be bad.but the capacity to create that chapter is on YOU.

TWO
QUESTIONS

of course you might get worry about your life, past will be regretfull and present will be empty but the thing is the past is your lesson and the present YOU gonna live and have joyness dont repeat the history because the lesson learned should never repeat!!

atlast future?eveytime yours thoughts,but never get stressed about it.change things in your present.

never judge yourself worthless or if other say its none you gonna hear it

THREE

TRUE INSPIRATION

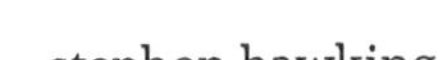

- stephen hawking
- albert einstein

stephen haw

He didn't close his mind when his body failed and today at the age of 73 while he was just given hardly anytime he proved that it's about the will to live and readiness to accept challenges. Death has to come but the life which we have between birth and death is up to us and it's our will how we want to live. As he says – "I'm not afraid of death, but I'm in no hurry to die." (Stephen Hawking)

story

He was born in 1942 in the month of January in Oxford, England. Incidentally, his family had moved due to the threat that V2 rockets posed to London. He was known in childhood too for his talent and unorthodox study methods. He studied at the University College, Oxford University where he studied Physics. Stephen Hawking was an extraordinary student according to his physics tutor Robert Berman. He was able to work out theorems and solutions in a unique manner that no one else could do. He got B.A. Hons in Physics and stayed briefly as he wanted to study astronomy. He later moved to Trinity College, Cambridge and was able to satisfy his passion for theoretical astronomy and cosmology. At Cambridge, he developed symptoms related to neuro-muscular problems which were a motor neuron disease. His physical movements were disrupted. The speech became slower and sluggish, and he became unable to even to feed himself. He was at one stage given lifespan of three years by the doctors.

Despite the latest technology being in use, it was a time-consuming process for Stephen Hawkins to communicate. His fields of research have been theoretical cosmology and quantum gravity and he was also able to develop a mathematical model for Albert Einstein's General Theory of Relativity. He also worked on the nature of the Universe, The Big Bang, and Black Hole theory.

.

<u>A SENSE OF HUMOR IS EVERYHING</u>:*Rather than be morose about his condition, Stephen Hawking chose to confront it head-on. He was a rather cheery and optimistic person and commonly appeared in various comedy shows and skits. One of these skits even showed him mowing another man down with his wheelchair. From the Simpsons to Futurama, and some comedy based talk shows, Hawking had guest appearances in them all.*

.

<u>Always strive to make a difference</u>"*Another dream I had several times was that I would sacrifice my life to save others. After all, if I was going to die anyway, I might as well do some good.*"*Part of a quote by Stephen*

Hawking, this shows his dedication towards the world. He focused on making complex scientific ideas more accessible to the general populace. His style of writing was 'Pop-science' that tried to generate a scientific way of thinking in people. Stephen Hawking wanted to contribute as much as he could towards the world. In his later life, he even worked on a TV Show called 'Genius' wherein ordinary people were asked questions about the universe and taught how to 'think like a genius'. He even worked on writing children's books with his daughter Lucy. These were designed to explain concepts of theoretical physics and other similar concepts in a simpler and more accessible manner.

albert einstein

Albert Einstein was born on March 14, 1879, in the city of Ulm, in the Kingdom of Württemberg in the German Empire. His parents lived in a very different world from what it is now: there was no electric light. The year Albert was born was the same year the electric bulb was invented by Thomas Edison. Albert was not a childhood prodigy. He started speaking relatively late when he was three years old. His parents made him see a doctor worrying that Albert had developmental issues.

As a student, young Einstein did not show remarkable results. Most of his grades were passing, and he was near the top of his class, but mainly because of math and science. In 1895, at the age of 16, Albert Einstein was determined to study electrical engineering, but he entered the Zürich Polytechnic (ETH Zurich) at the four-year mathematics and physics teaching diploma program at the age of 17. He skipped classes that he did not like and was a frequent guest in coffee houses and beer halls. To pass his exams, Albert copied class notes from Marcel Grossmann, which got him the highest grades in the group surpassing Grossmann himself. Einstein got some of his first ideas when still in college.

- When Albert Einstein was working in Princeton university, one day he was going back home he forgot his home address. The driver of the cab did not recognise him. Einstein asked the driver if he knows

Einstein's home. The driver said "Who does not know Einstein's address? Everyone in Princeton knows. Do you want to meet him? Einstein replied "I am Einstein. I forgot my home address, can you take me there? "The driver reached him to his home and did not even collect his fare from him.